LINDA'S LATE

A FUN BOOK OF TIME

First published in the U.S. in 1991 by
Carolrhoda Books, Inc.
All U.S. rights reserved. No part of this book may be
reproduced, stored in a retrieval system, or transmitted in
any form or by any means, electronic, mechanical,
photocopying, recording, or otherwise, without the prior
written permission of the Publisher except for the inclusion
of brief quotations in an acknowledged review.

Library of Congress Cataloging-in-Publication Data

Morris, Neil.
    Linda's late: a fun book of time /written by Neil Morris;
illustrated by Peter Stevenson.
        p.   cm.—(Fun books of learning)
    "First published in 1990 by Firefly Books Limited...East Sussex
...England"—T.p. verso.
    Summary: Follows, hour by hour, Linda's activities from the time
she gets up at seven o'clock in the morning to the time she goes to
bed at seven o'clock in the evening.
    ISBN 0-87614-675-2
    [1. Time—Fiction. 2. Day—Fiction.] I. Stevenson, Peter, 1953-
ill. II. Title. III. Series: Morris, Neil. Fun books of learning.
PZ7.M8284Li   1991
[E]—dc20   90-21122
                                                    CIP
                                                    AC

Printed in Italy by Rotolito Lombarda S.p.A., Milan

Bound in the United States of America

1 2 3 4 5 6 7 8 9 10 00 99 98 97 96 95 94 93 92 91

FUN BOOKS OF LEARNING

LINDA'S LATE

A FUN BOOK OF TIME

by Neil Morris
illustrated by Peter Stevenson

Carolrhoda Books, Inc./Minneapolis

"Wake up, Linda!" Mom says. "It's seven o'clock."

Linda gets dressed, but her toy rabbit is fast asleep.

"Wake up, Flat Rabbit," she says. "We shouldn't be late for breakfast."

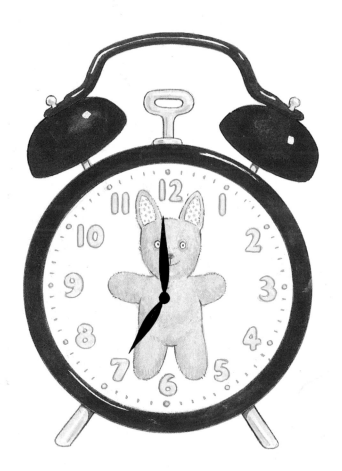

Eight o'clock is breakfast time.
"Where have you been?" George asks.
"You're late!"

Linda wants to take Flat Rabbit to nursery school, but now she can't find him. It's almost nine o'clock, so they have to hurry. They get to school just in time.

At ten o'clock, Mrs. Jones reads the children a story. Then she plays the piano, and they sing their favorite songs.

Eleven o'clock is painting time. Linda paints a picture of Flat Rabbit. She asks her teacher if she can take it home.

Mom always picks up Linda at twelve o'clock.
 Today she is a little late.

Lunch is at one o'clock. Linda has tomato soup.

"I wonder what George is having for lunch at school," Mom says.

Mom is expecting a visitor at two o'clock.
The visitor arrives early. They talk about
work while Linda looks at a book.

Linda has a tea party with her toys at three o'clock. She tries again to find Flat Rabbit.

"If Rabbit doesn't come soon, he'll miss the party," Linda tells her teddy bears.

George comes home from school at four
o'clock, but he doesn't want to play with Linda.
He's in a bad mood.

They watch television at five o'clock. Mom watches too, then falls asleep.

Mom goes jogging at six o'clock.
Linda shows Dad the picture
she painted at school.

Seven o'clock is Linda's bedtime. But she is still looking for her rabbit, and now she's late.

At last she finds him.

"You went to bed early, Flat Rabbit!" Linda says.

FUN BOOKS OF LEARNING

LINDA'S LATE
A Fun Book of Time

JUMP ALONG
A Fun Book of Movement

HOLLY AND HARRY
A Fun Book of Sizes

WHAT A NOISE
A Fun Book of Sounds

MAGIC MONKEY
A Fun Book of Numbers

I'M BIG
A Fun Book of Opposites

RUMMAGE SALE
A Fun Book of Shapes and Colors

FEEL!
A Fun Book of Touch